Paddington

MICHAEL BOND

and the
Christmas Surprise

ILLUSTRATED BY R.W. ALLEY

Collins

An Imprint of HarperCollins*Publishers*

First published by HarperCollins *Publishers*, USA in 1997. First published in Great Britain by Collins in 1997
Collins is an imprint of HarperCollins *Publishers* Ltd 77-85 Fulham Palace Road, Hammersmith, London, W6 8JB
1 3 5 7 9 8 6 4 2

Text copyright © Michael Bond 1997. Illustrations copyright © R.W. Alley 1997. ISBN 0 00 198285 0
Printed and bound in Singapore by Imago. All rights reserved.

One Christmas Paddington announced he was taking the Brown family to Barkridges store to see Santa Claus.

"It's very good value," he explained. "Apart from meeting Mr Claus, there's a sleigh ride through Winter

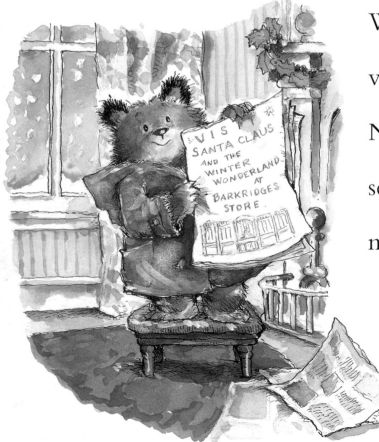

Wonderland and you get to visit his workshop at the North Pole. We might even see where he makes his marmalade."

"I doubt if Santa makes his own marmalade," said Mrs Brown nervously, as Paddington led the way onto the escalator.

"It would make all the presents sticky," agreed Jonathan.

"Not to mention his beard," added Judy. "Besides, he's much too busy."

"That's more than you can say for Barkridges," remarked Mr Brown gloomily, as he brought up the rear. "There's hardly anyone here."

There were two signs at the top of the escalator, one pointing to Santa Claus, and one pointing to Winter Wonderland.

"I think I may visit Santa Claus first," announced Paddington, "in case the sleigh gets stuck in the snow."

"You're supposed to do it the other way round, dear," called Mrs Brown. "You don't want to miss the ride."

But Paddington was already in the queue.

There were only two children in front of him and they were both rather large, so he got down on his paws and knees so that he could get a better look.

Santa Claus had two sacks of presents. One was marked BOYS and the other was marked GIRLS, but he couldn't see a sack marked BEARS anywhere.

Just then he looked up and saw

a man staring down at him.

"Are you a boy or a girl?" asked the

store manager.

"I'm neither," said Paddington. "I'm a bear."

"You look more like a large creepy-crawly

to me," said the man distastefully. "Perhaps you had better

come back next year when you've made up your mind."

"Come back next year," repeated

Paddington hotly. "But I've brought my

Christmas list. I thought it would save

the postage."

The Browns were too far away to hear what was being said, but from the look on Paddington's face they guessed something must be wrong.

"Hurry up," called Mrs Bird. "We're all ready to go."

"Oh dear, Henry," said Mrs Brown. "I do hope the sleigh ride is a success. Paddington's been saving his bun money for ages and he'll be most upset if it doesn't live up to his expectations."

As Paddington clambered aboard and they set off, Mr Brown held up a leaflet. "Listen everybody," he called. "First of all, we go past Santa's winter garden."

"I think I prefer Mrs Bird's window box," said Paddington.

The Browns exchanged anxious glances. It didn't seem a very good start to the outing.

"How about this one, then?" continued Mr Brown, as they turned a corner. "It's the stable where Santa keeps his reindeer."

Paddington didn't say anything. From where he was sitting it looked more like a dog kennel, and the only reindeer he could see was a plastic one that had fallen over in the snow.

Next, Mr Brown pointed to a very tall tower with a flashing light at the top. "That's the lighthouse at the North Pole," he said. "It's there to make sure Santa arrives back home safe and sound after he's delivered all his presents."

Paddington gave it a hard stare. "I think there must be a wire loose, Mr Brown," he exclaimed. "The light keeps going on and off."

"Lighthouses are supposed to flash," broke in Jonathan. "They all send out a different signal so that people know exactly where they are."

But Paddington wasn't listening. He was counting the number of buns it had taken to pay for the outing.

The North Pole.

"Now, this might be more interesting." Mr Brown tried to strike a cheerful note as they drew nearer to a big house with mechanical figures moving behind every window. "We're about to enter Santa's workshop."

"Look at all the elves," called Judy.

She turned round in order to explain elves to Paddington, but as she did so she gave a cry of alarm, for he was nowhere to be seen.

"Do something, Henry!" cried Mrs Brown when she saw what had happened.

"Do something?" repeated Mr Brown. "What can I do from inside the middle of a workshop?"

"We haven't reached the end of the tour," warned Mrs Bird. "Paddington will be most upset if he misses any of it."

As the manager disappeared through one door, Paddington came through another.

"I think I've found the fault in the lighthouse, Mr Brown," he called. "Bears are good at mending things and…"

But before he had a chance to finish there was a loud bang from somewhere inside Santa's workshop, and all the lights went out.

"Where is he?" shouted the manager. "Where is he? I'll give him a present he won't forget in a hurry!"

Mrs Bird took a firm grip of her umbrella.

"Come along, everyone," she called. "I think we've had enough wonders for one day."

"Paddington's certainly hit the headlines," said Mr Brown at breakfast the next morning. "Listen to this: 'Strange Goings-on in London Store'."

"One thing's certain," said Mrs Brown. "We shan't be allowed into Barkridges again in a hurry."

"I don't know," broke in Jonathan. "Listen to this one: 'Crowds Flock to Santa's Workshop. Search for Mystery Bear Goes On'."

Everyone was so busy reading the newspapers that they didn't notice Mrs Bird leave the room. She had an important telephone call to make.

"Barkridges," said the manager, several days later, "wishes you all a very Merry Christmas. Ever since this young bear first honoured us with a visit we've had queues outside our store. It's quite like old times."

He turned to Mrs Bird. "And thank you, dear lady, for telephoning us when you did."

"Perhaps I could do some more repairs for you?" said Paddington hopefully.

"I don't think that will be necessary," said the manager hastily. "Besides, Santa is waiting to see you. After you've all had a free sleigh ride."

It was a merry party of Browns who set off on their journey through Winter Wonderland. This time everything worked perfectly, and when they came to the end of the ride Santa Claus was waiting to greet them.

"Ho ho ho," he boomed. "And who have we here?"

"I'm a bear, Mr Claus," said Paddington. "And I come from Darkest Peru."

"Well," said Santa, reaching behind his chair, "in that case I think I know just what you would like."

Paddington nearly fell over backwards with surprise as Santa Claus held up an enormous jar. There was a label on the side that said HOME-MADE and it was tied at the top with a big red bow.

"It's my favourite, Mr Claus!" he cried. "How did you guess?"

Mrs Bird's face went pink as Santa gave her a knowing smile. "One of the nice things about Santa Claus," she said hastily, "is that he knows exactly what everyone wants for Christmas. That's what makes him so special."

"And he makes his own marmalade," said Paddington happily. "I knew he would!"